# MY

# IS THE MOST

# WOMAN IN

*A Russian Folktale*
*Retold by* BECKY REYHER

# MOTHER

# BEAUTIFUL

# THE WORLD

*Pictures by*

*RUTH GANNETT*

LOTHROP, LEE & SHEPARD CO., INC.

"We do not love people because they are beautiful,
but they seem beautiful to us because we love them!"

—an old Russian proverb

Once upon a time, long, long ago, when the harvest season had come again in the Ukraine, the villagers were all busy cutting and gathering the wheat. For this is the land from which most Russians get the flour for their bread.

Marfa and Ivan went to the field early each day, as did all their children. There they stayed until sundown. Varya was Marfa's and Ivan's youngest little girl, six years old. When everyone went to the fields in harvest time, Varya went, too. Her legs were so short she had to run and skip to keep up with her mother's and father's long steps.

"Varyachka, you are a little slow poke!" her father said to her. Then, laughing loudly, he swung her up on his shoulder where she had to hold tight to his neck, for his arms were full carrying the day's lunch and the long scythe to cut the wheat.

In the field, in the long even rows between the thick wheat, Varya knew just what she must do. First, she must stay at least twenty or thirty paces behind her father, who now took even greater and bigger steps, so that he might have plenty of room to swing wide the newly sharpened scythe.

'Stand back, Varyachka! Mind the scythe!" her father warned. Swish, swish, swish, went his even strokes, and down came the wheat, faster and faster, as he made his great strides.

Soon Marfa began to follow Ivan. She gathered the wheat in sheaves or bunches just big enough to bind together with a strand of braided wheat. Varya, eager to be useful, helped gather the wheat, and held each bunch while her mother tied it. When three sheaves were tied, they were stacked against each other in a little pyramid.

"Careful, Varyachka!" her mother cautioned, "the wheat side up!"

After a while, instead of long rows of wheat, there were long rows of sheaves, standing stiffly.

Sometimes Varya forgot to follow her mother. On very hot days she stopped to rest upon the warm ground, and let her tired, bare feet and toes tickle the dark, moist earth. A while later she ran and caught up with her mother, and then her mother hugged her to her and wiped her dripping face. Even though her mother's arms and bosom were hot and damp, they felt cool and restful to Varya.

Day after day, Ivan, Marfa, and Varya, went to the field, until all the wheat was cut and stacked and none was left growing in the ground. Then a big wagon came and everyone pitched the wheat up to the driver who packed it in solidly, and carefully, and took it to the threshing barn.

When the harvest was over, Ivan, Marfa, Varya, and everyone in the village prepared for the feast day. And what a feast they had!

The Russian sun shines with a warm glow that makes Russia's wheat the most nourishing in the world, and her fruit and vegetables the most delicious that ever grew. The cherries are the reddest, largest and juiciest, the apples the firmest and crunchiest to the teeth, the cucum-

bers the most plentiful on the vine. As for the watermelons, only someone who has seen a Ukrainian watermelon really knows what watermelons should be.

The villagers worked tirelessly throughout the summer. Their muscles ached, but there was a song in their hearts, and there were merry chuckles on their lips. Hard work produced a rich harvest. There would be wheat for everybody. It was time, then, for a grand celebration.

When Varya was five years old, a year ago, she was allowed to share in the excitement of preparing the feast. That summer she helped her mother bake the little cakes of plaited flat dough, stuffed with meat or cabbage. *Piroghki*, they were called.

When all the cakes were rolled out, Varya's mother said: "And for you, Varyachka, a special one, a *piroghochok*." That meant, in Russian, a darling little cake. It also meant that harvest day was a holiday, and that Varya's busy mother could take the time to bake a special cake for her.

Besides the *piroghki*, Varya and her mother brought *blini* to the feast. These are flat, rolled, browned, little pancakes, filled almost to bursting, with jelly or cheese. They are eaten smothered with thick cream, or plain, held between sticky fingers.

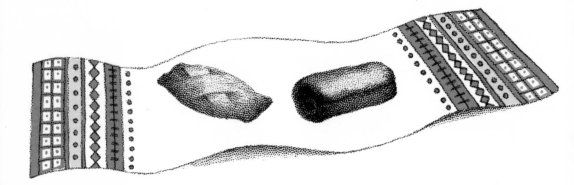

Varya had taken her turn at rolling out the dough for the *piroghki,* for the thinner the dough, the lighter the *piroghki.* This was one of the housewifely lessons she had to master.

The feast always took place after church in the very heart of the village. Varya came with her parents. Everybody was there. The grandmothers whom Russians call Baboushka, and who always wear a gay kerchief tied below their chin. The mothers with babies in their arms. The strong, broad-shouldered fathers. And the many children, all with roses in their cheeks.

Tolya, the village leader, played the accordion. The minute his music started, everybody's feet began to keep time. The boys whistled, and stamped their feet, and everybody clapped their hands.

Tolya stood in the center, all eyes upon him. He danced a jigging step or two, his fingers never leaving the accordion, and shouted: "Too quiet, my friends. A little more nonsense. A little more noise. A few more smiles. Sing! Sing! My friends, this is a holiday! Come! Everyone on their feet! We must have a dance!"

Men, women, and children joined in the singing, as Tolya swung his accordion into rollicking dance tunes.

The men wore polished knee high, heavy boots, but they danced as if their feet were bare. As the music grew faster and faster, their feet grew lighter and nimbler. It was as if they and their partners had wings that carried them swiftly by those who were watching. To Varya it seemed that the older girls' braids flew by like birds in the wind.

The girls wore lots of petticoats under a skirt so wide you could not tell where it began, or where it ended. Around their necks were many strings of beads that shone as bright as a Christmas tree, all tied with trailing strings of many colored ribbons.

Some of the little girls were dressed almost as grandly. But not Varya, nor most of them.

Varya kept asking her mother: "When am I going to have a beautiful dance costume with lots of beads?"

And Varya's mother would say: "When you are a grown up young lady, Varya."

Always it seemed to Varya she just could not wait until she was grown up.

Varya was an impatient little girl. Her impatience was like a teasing toothache. Today it was so great she felt choked, as if she had swallowed a whole watermelon. For today was the last day for gathering the wheat. By evening all the wheat would be cut, stacked in pyramids, and waiting for the wagon to take it to the threshing barn. Tomorrow another wonderful feast day and celebration would come around again. Varya could hardly wait for the feast day to begin.

Bright and early Marfa, Ivan, and Varya went to the wheat field. "We must get to it," warned Ivan, "this is our last day to get the wheat in!"

"It has been a good crop, Ivan, hasn't it?" asked Marfa.

"Indeed, yes!" Ivan answered heartily, "And it will mean a good warm winter with plenty to eat. We have much to be thankful for."

Marfa and Ivan worked quicker and harder than ever. They did not seem to notice the hot sun. The wheat swished almost savagely as it came rushing down.

But to Varya the day seemed the longest she had ever lived. The sun seemed hotter than on any other day, and her feet seemed almost too heavy to lift.

Varya peered into the next row of wheat which was not yet cut. There it was cool and pleasant and the sun did not bear down with its almost unbearable heat. Varya moved in just a little further to surround herself with that blessed coolness. "How lucky I am!" she thought, "to be able to hide away from the hot sun. I will do this for just a few minutes. Surely Mamochka will not mind if I do not help her all the day."

Soon Varya grew sleepy, for in so cool a place, one could curl up and be very quiet and comfortable.

When Varya woke, she jumped to her feet and started to run toward her mother. But her mother was nowhere in sight.

Varya called, "Mama," "Mama," "Mamochka," but there was no answer.

Sometimes her mother got ahead of her and was so busy with her work she did not hear.

"Maybe if I run along the row, I will catch up with her," Varya thought.

She ran and ran,
and soon she was out of breath, but
nowhere could she see her mother.

"Maybe I have gone in the wrong direction," she said
to herself. So she ran the other way. But here, too, there
was no trace of her mother.

Varya was alone in the wheat fields, where she could
see nothing but tall pyramids of wheat towering above
her. When she called out, her voice brought no response,
no help. Overhead the sun was not so bright as it had
been. Varya knew that soon it would be night and that
she must find her mother.

Varya cut through the last of the wheat that had not yet been cut, breaking her own pathway, which bent and hurt the wheat. She would not have done this, had she not been frightened.

When it was almost dark, Varya stumbled into a clearing where several men and women had paused to gossip after the day's work. It took her only a second to see that these were strangers, and that neither her mother nor father were among them.

The little girl stared ahead of her, not knowing what to do. One of the men spied her and said in a booming voice which he thought was friendly, "Look what we have here!"

Everyone turned to Varya. She was sorry that with so many strangers looking at her, she had her hair caught back in a tiny braid with a bit of string, and that she was wearing only her oldest, most faded dress. Surely, too, by now her face and hands must be as streaked with dirt as were her legs and dress. This made her burst into tears.

"Poor little thing," cried one of the women, putting her arms around Varya, "she is lost!" But this sympathy, and the strange voices made Varya want her mother all the more. She could not help crying.

"We must know her name, and the name of her mother and father. Then we can unite them," said the women.

"Little girl, little girl," they said, "what is your name? What is your mother's and father's name?" But Varya was too unhappy to speak.

Finally because her longing for her mother was so great, she sobbed out:

"*My mother is the most beautiful woman in the world!*"

All the men and women smiled. The tallest man, Kolya, clapped his hands and laughingly said, "*Now we have something to go on.*"

This was long, long ago, when there were no telephones and no automobiles. If people wanted to see each other, or carry a message, they went on their two feet.

From every direction, friendly, good-hearted boys ran to village homes with orders to bring back the beautiful women.

"Bring Katya, Manya, Vyera, Nadya," the tall man, Kolya, called to one boy.

"Ay, but don't forget the beauty, Lisa," he called to still another boy.

The women came running. These were orders from
Kolya, the village leader. Also the mothers, who had left
the fields early to get supper for their families, thought
perhaps this was indeed their child who was lost.

As each beautiful woman came rushing up, blushing
and proud that she had been so chosen, Kolya would say
to her: "We have a little lost one here. Stand back, everyone, while the little one tells us if this is her mother!"

The mothers laughed and pushed, and called to
Kolya: "You big tease! What about asking each mother
if this is her child? We know our children!"

To Varya this was very serious, for she was lost and she was desperate without her mother. As she looked at each strange woman, Varya shook her head in disappointment and sobbed harder. Soon every known beauty from far and near, from distances much further than a child could have strayed, had come and gone. Not one of them was Varya's mother.

The villagers were really worried. They shook their heads. Kolya spoke for them. "One of us will have to take the little one home for the night. Tomorrow may bring fresh wisdom to guide us!"

Just then a breathless, excited woman came puffing up to the crowd. Her face was big and broad, and her body even larger. Her eyes were little pale slits between a great lump of a nose. The mouth was almost toothless. Even as a young girl everyone had said, "A homely girl like Marfa is lucky to get a good husband like Ivan."

"Varyachka!" cried this woman.

"Mamochka!" cried the little girl, and they fell into each other's arms. The two of them beamed upon each other. Varya cuddled into that ample and familiar bosom. The smile Varya had longed for was once again shining upon her.

All of the villagers smiled thankfully when Varya looked up from her mother's shoulder and said with joy:

*"This is my mother! I told you my mother is the most beautiful woman in the world!"*

The group of friends and neighbors, too, beamed upon each other, as Kolya repeated the proverb so well known to them, a proverb which little Varya had just proved: *"We do not love people because they are beautiful, but they seem beautiful to us because we love them."*

Next day was the feast day. In the evening Varya sat cuddled in her mother's lap, and happily watched the dancing. As the music played, she brought her mother's head close to her own and whispered: "Mamochka, the dancers, they are so beautiful. I love to watch them."

Her mother patted Varya and whispered back: "This is the harvest feast day. Everyone is wearing their best clothes, and their best smile. Of course it is fun to watch them!"

Varya was so happy and felt so safe, she was able to speak of the dark, awful moments when she was lost.

"Mamochka," she said, haltingly, as if she could not find the right words, "Some of the children have teased me. They laughed about my calling you the most beautiful woman in the world. They say the angels, the Czarina, the Princesses, the Queens, the rich, their own mothers, are the most beautiful. One of *them* is the most beautiful woman in the world."

"Mamochka," Varya went on, "I know that some of those women have more beads than you. Some have bigger and wider skirts. Maybe some of them can sing and dance better than you can. But, Mamochka, to me, you are the most beautiful woman in the world!"

Varya's mother, Marfa, kissed her, smiled happily and said: "Some people, Varyachka, see with their eyes alone. Others see with their hearts, too. I am grateful and lucky that you see with your heart, as well as with your eyes."

In this frame you may place
a picture of your own mother—
The Most Beautiful Woman In The World

"Ho ho!" cried the little boy, running through the foamy water.
"I was here first! I was the very first one.
I saw the sea come in!"
And with the long strong feather he wrote his name

TIMOTHY ROBBINS
in the firm damp white sand in front of the sliding water.

And as the high tide waves swept over the beach the people
with their beach towels and umbrellas skittered back out of the way.
Just like the sandpipers.

But the waves rose higher than the walls,
and the sea took back the sandhopper.

and a very fine castle it was...
with a seaweed banner floating from the tallest tower...
with a sandhopper for a captive princess in the courtyard...
with a moat and a drawbridge to protect her from enemies.

"Now I will be a knight and build a castle here in the sand,"
said the little boy.
"I will build high towers and a wall to stop the sea."
With his pail he made towers, and with his hands he made walls,

Past a funny old man reading a newspaper.
Past a leathery horseshoe crab on his slow way back to the waves.
Past a fisherman casting for blue fish in the foaming water.
While the new tide crept higher and higher on the beach.

The little boy picked up a long bird's feather, long and strong.
Just right for a wild Indian.
But it was gray like the fog and the sea gulls.
Not red or yellow like an Indian war whoop.
So he tucked it in his captain's cap and trudged on down the beach

And still the rising tide crept higher and higher up the sandy shore.
Now the sun came out and the gray fog melted away.
Now boats with white sails bobbed in the blue water.
Now the beach was gay with big umbrellas.

He found a conch shell, spiraled pink and white.
And the conch shell sang its sea song to his ear.
He found a star fish and a hermit crab,
and he popped them in his pail.

"Nobody has ever been here before me!" he cried.
"I am the first one!"
He tied his handkerchief to the handle of the shovel
for a flag, and he stuck it in the sand.

And the little boy set off down the lonely white beach, while minute by minute, wave by wave, the new tide crept up the sandy shore.

The little boy looked up the beach
but all he could see was sea mist and fog.
"I will be an explorer," he said. "I will find the end of the beach."

Clink, watch out ... clank, take care.
Clink, watch out ... clank, take care.
The gray sea gulls floated overhead in the soft gray fog.
Scree ... scree ... scree ...
Then down they swooped to scoop a fish from the waves.

He heard the fog horn booming, deep and strong,
from the lightship far out in the water.
Rocks...beware, rocks...beware, rocks...beware.
Then he heard the bell buoys clank as they bobbled in the waves.

Only pale fragile sandhoppers hopping.
Just a clam blowing bubbles up through the wet sand.
And the little boy was happy because he was the first one.

Only a skittery sandpiper
puttering along the lacy edge of the waves.
Only a spindly-legged crab crawling sideways to the sea.

And nobody was there because the little boy was the first one.

Across the moors, past the spicy wild roses...
over a bank covered with whispering beach grasses...
slithering down through the slippery sand of a sand dune...
down went the little boy to the sea,
just as a new tide started its journey up the broad white beach.

He carried a pail to hold things.
He rested a shovel on his shoulder for digging.
And he wore an old cap on his head
to make him look like a sea captain.

Early in the morning, while the soft gray fog
still hung in the sky,
the little boy went down to the sea.

# THE SEA
# IN

by ALVIN TRESSELT

*illustrated by*

ROGER DUVOISIN

LOTHROP, LEE & SHEPARD CO., INC. • NEW YORK